Not A Wake

A Dream

*Embodying π's digits fully
for 10000 decimals*

Michael Keith

Illustrated by
Diana Keith

Vinculum Press • 3/14/10

The first three-quarters of section one (up to the row of asterisks) first appeared under the title "Octopi" in the magazine *Word Ways*, Volume 42, No. 1, Feb. 2009. Permission to reprint is gratefully acknowledged.

π

3141592653 5897932384 6264338327 9502884197 1693993751
0582097494 4592307816 4062862089 9862803482 5342117067
9821480865 1328230664 7093844609 5505822317 2535940812
8481117450 2841027019 3852110555 9644622948 9549303819
6442881097 5665933446 1284756482 3378678316 5271201909
1456485669 2346034861 0454326648 2133936072 6024914127
3724587006 6063155881 7488152092 0962829254 0917153643
6789259036 0011330530 5488204665 2138414695 1941511609
4330572703 6575959195 3092186117 3819326117 9310511854
8074462379 9627495673 5188575272 4891227938 1830119491
2983367336 2440656643 0860213949 4639522473 7190702179
8609437027 7053921717 6293176752 3846748184 6766940513
2000568127 1452635608 2778577134 2757789609 1736371787
2146844090 1224953430 1465495853 7105079227 9689258923
5420199561 1212902196 0864034418 1598136297 7477130996
0518707211 3499999983 7297804995 1059731732 8160963185
9502445945 5346908302 6425223082 5334468503 5261931188
1710100031 3783875288 6587533208 3814206171 7766914730
3598253490 4287554687 3115956286 3882353787 5937519577
8185778053 2171226806 6130019278 7661119590 9216420198

Now I fall, a tired suburbian in liquid under the trees
Drifting alongside forests simmering red in the twilight over Europe.
So scream with the old mischief, ask me another conundrum
About bitterness of possible fortunes near a landscape Italian.
A little happiness may sometimes intervene but usually fades.
A missionary cries, striving to understand worthless, tedious life.
Monotony's lost amid ocean movements
As the bewildered sailors hesitate. I become salt,
Submerging people in dazzling oceans of enshrouded unbelief.
Christmas ornaments conspire.
Beauty is, somewhat inevitably now, both
Feelings of faith and eyes of rationalism.

Blinded delusional horses stumble;
Facetious nonsense is a dark, secluded tabernacle.
Comfort's buried: bleed a bit as antidote. Is one recovering?
Verily, octopi sing:
Burning choristers accompany the mournful song.
Don't ponder constantly – existence waits,
Among sunsetting tones, bringing it to you.
A wedding of birds and boars compounds with disloyalty,
Devising contemporary treasons.
This morning's displeasure: a badger's life ended,
Frightened to roadkill when a procession of hearses approached.
I whispered the profound truth of symmetrical restraints:
Untie every chain, sacrifice belief, free each beggar,
Go to everybody with peaceful, beautiful hands.

From stairways the multitudes fly downward,
A pointless heaven-like hell to conceive together.
A tourniquet-enwrapped servant walks beside Dover's beach,
Creatures cut the skin deep within a so-infinite void.

Fragile trees gently sway, buffeted by the odd paradox,
Colorful grassy meadows describe sin.
I pursue truth as heaven's kaleidoscope constructs a slideshow:
"Consistent Universes: A Myth-Taken Notion."
This ethereal bliss points toward emptiness,
To the hour whence suppertime has fled.
Creation offers a motionless, cold world.
Look now to crimes around city boroughs
To a new way, forgiving all thirty complaints.

Rejoice as queens distribute to poor commoners,
A lamp illuminating faintly the corners of each house.
Imperial sultans annihilate themselves inside palace fortresses;
Within ice a vine's quiet creeping imitates a classic tale.
Everyone realizes a heart is overdosing somewhere
As porcupinal emissions submit to medicine.
So whereupon is color fled? Everywhere, elsewhere.
A journal: a life's odd purple inks and shabby volumes,
Ignorant scribbles of minor hardships.
Portfolios and crates discourage betterment,
Considering the way presidents filed and squandered truth.
Have swinging treetops my bootstraps? Have bushes cherry kites?
No, I see blossoms.

Make a fire across spreading waves:
A forgotten play, a dance transferred,
Paving blackstone hillsides with the old bloodlines.
Shoes encased in travels congregate, not moving,
While funeral-feast escapades waste sentiment.
I disappear under the horrifying nightmare in a measured manner,
Brightening candles set phantoms a-scuttling off my window,
Materialism battles knowledge. Why?

A xylophone's bells crystallize thoughts about salt monsters:
Childhood's terrors live deep inside, in the closets,
Imaginary incidents simmer in Samson's head.
Nighttime dream beside streams and waves:
A scouring scorpion steps through.
Watch me. Sustain me.

Your serenity resembles nightingales on girders, deathless and tranquil.
I retrieve the farsighted pharmacist's tasteless pill,
Garnering disconcerted approvals.
Amputate the old hearts, implant the new hearts
In your head, tarnishing plates under silver.
Please take the headstrong shilling,
Please compensate me a bit alongside kind strangers.
Don't impart our syndromes again to my kids.
Sodium's the element a difficult experience demands,
Tenderness is a theorem disproven entirely.
Repeat childhood's senseless song,
Say goodbye/hallelujah to parable, romance, headstones.
Smash the whirlwind to a silence, a silence bereft of heartache.
Now, a silence.

Dreams release songs, so hum freedom's song.
Squash insects that disquiet a luncheon food spread,
Silence velvet-ridden screaming.
Hear springtime birds, a day of burlesqued buttercups.
Bejewelled maids wander randomly,
Increasingly aimless (a love lyric is better for tears).
Earth's sauntering traveler is feeding, feeding everyone agony,
Feeding himself a bad diet of safaris among nuclear changes.
Pinpoint notebooks whilst cuttlefish establish a pattern;
The London Eye watches.

A fishing mongoose springs as a tuna passes archways from hell,
Forgivable frailties forgetting.
Transforming my well-appointed dream not long off,
Discordant I sing.

Echoes: shoes upon ambulance floor, sickness above the ceiling.
A confidante feels vibrations, ignores durations.
As an evening dissolves, undead humanity
Commences to float westward, televised to the world.
With no compassion I speculate regarding these events,
Undermining my significance, muttering:
Dependence is a whimsical hatred,
Turbulence enlarges others' pain,
Conscience may fail like a bludgeon.
A wind's streaming launches a cat across my landscape,
Falling, falling down, falling, falling.
I see worshipers embracing weathered stones,
Recounting ideas I suddenly retrace:
Collective courage is everlasting, its core
Blameless, bloodless, guiltless, ceaseless, limitless, boundless.

*   *   *   *   *   *   *   *

Remember, it's nothing of ourselves:
Without wounding countrymen we're subjected.
Happiness which I restricted grows,
Considers mankind and a recluse now in defiance.
A shadow emphasizes existence.
Africa, see a promised manna somewhere under prophesies.
So come with ideas, gentlemen, when their roots are good enough,
Nurturing distressed humanity.
For insulation, my turban acts as armor;
It is not impossible.

5

Question my heart for its rust, hold purity somewhat ahead:
Everybody's God, small as nearly a desperate man,
Frequenting warrior's basement o' weapons.
I conjecture I understand everything:
Colleagues and I can inspire together the creation forming there,
So renounce movement beyond death.

Computer support would not now be reasonable:
Kindness and passions I wish to accumulate,
Amidst a feeling, a strange emotion, seized within.
Formulate a time, perhaps for inevitably bad films
Regarding noblemen of Spain cut down summarily.
Understand what he deserved: France's chief acted with reason.

Suddenly towards the blacksmith's house presently sixty ladies go,
Debating events and partisan religion,
Or the other, the eternal question:
Whither goeth invisible God?

Passing North, I hesitated, after hearing fearful whispers.
I recalled those murmurs: another calamity overtaking faith,
God on a nominal technicality in winter repelled.
Prosperous people create a cry cheerfully,
Appointing a commander to worship effigies carried before dinner.
Celebrating a visionary vixen undressed gracefully,
Beautiful as a flower upon an octahedron, a statuette Thaleian.

9380952572 0106548586 3278865936 1533818279 6823030195
2035301852 9689957736 2259941389 1249721775 2834791315
1557485724 2454150695 9508295331 1686172785 5889075098
3817546374 6493931925 5060400927 7016711390 0984882401
2858361603 5637076601 0471018194 2955596198 9467678374
4944825537 9774726847 1040475346 4620804668 4259069491
2933136770 2898915210 4752162056 9660240580 3815019351
1253382430 0355876402 4749647326 3914199272 6042699227
9678235478 1636009341 7216412199 2458631503 0286182974
5557067498 3850549458 8586926995 6909272107 9750930295
5321165344 9872027559 6023648066 5499119881 8347977535
6636980742 6542527862 5518184175 7467289097 7772793800
0816470600 1614524919 2173217214 7723501414 4197356854
8161361157 3525521334 7574184946 8438523323 9073941433
3454776241 6862518983 5694855620 9921922218 4272550254
2568876717 9049460165 3466804988 6272327917 8608578438
3827967976 6814541009 5388378636 0950680064 2251252051
1739298489 6084128488 6269456042 4196528502 2210661186
3067442786 2203919494 5047123713 7869609563 6437191728
7467764657 5739624138 9086583264 5995813390 4780275900

PURGATORY

The monsters diligently collected water in their descent to Netherland. A remarkable mother named Rose followed close, silently spying and in despair stifling startled, buried cries. Zealously she sought a child: her one blessing, a moonbeam of comfort rebutting failed language of men, sufficient for overcoming a sorrowful heart. On throughout the south she confronted a terrible swarm of anomalies: giants, headless creatures, festering flesh, ghastly harpies, and scenes of an adult character.

"Afternoon, Rose," a dim phantasm whispered, bloodstained with liquefied scarlet in a thicket planted there. No elements did Rose observe excepting a cry, a snake, a quiet blood-gelling hiss. Sleeping pests blinked to life to tear flesh, make a break, everything devour. Sergeants tried radiation, began determined research in chromatic radio EMR for comparisons. Twenty spectres eluded a platoon to emanate piloting large tanks. Broadway rejected governing principles, steeled their unlawfully disturbed cemetery for conflict.

I brought forth this valley and rescued them, giving them something yet invisible. And I announced to every heart: scientific search reasonably made overthrows government autocracy. An awkward silence transpired. I simply laughed.

THEOLOGISTS

The penitents considered impossible existence, reverent acts crowding together in each experience. Intellectual disputes often occurred, but surely I cannot positively say where. Nobody did promise friendship. Because people seemed interested, I discovered this outside: a clattering, a clashing, a clamorous tone. It resembled their grief, ended gradually beyond. I therefore departed cordially, then during fifteen-visits thought occurred one another: from man's lassitude goes many failings. To quiet guilt one apostle lacerated himself; another went outside to lament, enduring some disease (a misfortune most mysterious). None reposed until his mind conned some crisis he remembered suddenly. Artificial hope curved around battered time to avoid offending. Expectancy filled believers, with moonlight consequences resulting.

And now a man drinks rapidly, fearing afterwards an abstruse gentlemen standing alongside, a child of a conception long expired. Death is a matter to dishearten every feeble scribbler, though heaven (infinitely of blue pasteboard boxes) prevails, sufficient for intrigue. I touch landscapes, a menagerie and large habitations of brick. For any inclined to vice, his invariably widespread net opens. Dusks engender mocking images, like literature in wine bottles with fireflies. Native gods surpass man in virtue, and everyone's a fool. I persevere.

IMPERFECT

He reaches it, before everything else, as winter convulses. Dismounts at it. Breezes penetrate deeply through overcoat in the sharp cold. Revenge imitates a desert, his spirit infuriated. Everything embitters him, from a fighter to a friend. When conversation a departure indicated, he left home's terrible secret. Now a large, melancholy God-marionette is situated nearby. A monument to greatness Anahman sees, there among blood-spotted engravings. "Indeed," Anahman says seriously.

Silently he's watching, these assurances being most unhelpful. Some water splashes downward among wisteria-draped figurines. He wishes something privately, while flying creatures accelerate northward in disgust. He (a-struggling against instantly nervous hands) alternates earthward and heavenward, to recognize ideas faded out of countenance, crying aloud: "Who knew? What substance? Whoever's causing my calamities?"

An ancient ivory knife summarily shines, unsheathed, it too crying "Life therein's punishment enough!" London smoke goes southward, repressed, uncertainly answering nothings. Suspense. A startled owl that shrieks forthwith enables courage. Knife and wrist commit coitus, the bloody discharge drowning everything between them. He smiles, falls, dies.

GO WITHE ME

Grandma provides things to these twins: a porridge, a luncheon, then a bedtime story, glowing fire, pillow. Instead of assuming affection originates naturally, Grandma sweetly, proudly fosters it. Grandma, seriously and entirely celebrated everywhere, constantly whistles a little song. Unhappy youngsters become captivated, resembling a family. A real feast of love, recalling a Christmas or a Holiday.

Now is a sunrise. On a sofa Grandma suffers – so old, faint, motionless. "O help! O!", they sigh, "O!" Overcoats gripped, the brave youths unfasten their door, entering a tumult: a day having destructive winds, showers, and snows. We might watch as a sad and worn peddler named Theodor with a gigantic pack struggles over Howth's enormous hill. The children hurry to him and, by the cavernous embankment, relieve his weariness. "What a lift!" the old man says, happy.

They journey through fields to view a little greenish hamlet in which a relative agreeably travails and lives. Hellos alternate. Rain produces fruit.

March brings an unexpected character, identical to a puppeteer, or to me. (I ofttimes like to perform, or mimic human melodramas.) To charm them he talks, dances, recounts Medieval legends. Before noonday a curious, deafening steamship's horn surprises them. Amidst expectancy, a ladder drops.

It's Papa, beside Mother! Children reacquaint with parentage, assemble together within an edifice or two. To endless inquiries a smiling helpmate pleads, "Afterwards. Somebody, bring Mother's children here!"

THE SOLDIERS

Mud. Promises of letters. Footfalls before sunrise. Countless corpses within fallen barracks. A word blown into a conspiracy, threatened expulsion, bombs for mindless promises, and escaped hostages during the winter initiative. Opponents hatch strategies during Saturday congresses, resistance urging them on. As quick intelligence would be altogether wrong, penetration through the religious or political discords have affected everybody. Battle undermines kindness.

This outspreading reproach from assigned agencies, whilst we amused ourselves, made quite little difference. Here is such a nightmare beyond sleep, an illusion quite fathomless. As we go I reconsider myself. Should passiveness engender strife, and continents divide, leading from that to Empress opposing Prince in an engagement for supremacy? I speculate that something here makes executions seem ethical – peradventure the goddess I had spotted towering within sanctuary groves.

Throughout warfaring zones marine and gunner take his station. I recollect a passage in Pushkin's *Gypsies*. Capt. Antony Stewart sternly passes from before their current ruler, equally his indignity arisen as that I had formerly. Languidly, resembling balloons rising under carnival sky, an atomic bomb flies, alighting ravishing fires. Ashpiles I had not predicted degenerate into airless infinity.

Everything is carrion flesh. Conclusus. Benedicite. Benedicite.

π π π

9946576407 8951269468 3983525957 0982582262 0522489407
7267194782 6848260147 6990902640 1363944374 5530506820
3496252451 7493996514 3142980919 0659250937 2216964615
1570985838 7410597885 9597729754 9893016175 3928468138
2686838689 4277415599 1855925245 9539594310 4997252468
0845987273 6446958486 5383673622 2626099124 6080512438
8439045124 4136549762 7807977156 9143599770 0129616089
4416948685 5584840635 3422072225 8284886481 5845602850
6016842739 4522674676 7889525213 8522549954 6667278239
8645659611 6354886230 5774564980 3559363456 8174324112
5150760694 7945109659 6094025228 8797108931 4566913686
7228748940 5601015033 0861792868 0920874760 9178249385
8900971490 9675985261 3655497818 9312978482 1682998948
7226588048 5756401427 0477555132 3796414515 2374623436
4542858444 7952658678 2105114135 4735739523 1134271661
0213596953 6231442952 4849371871 1014576540 3590279934
4037420073 1057853906 2198387447 8084784896 8332144571
3868751943 5064302184 5319104848 1005370614 6806749192
7819119793 9952061419 6634287544 4064374512 3718192179
9983910159 1956181467 5142691239 7489409071 8649423196

beautiful dwellings
upon silent hills,
   flowers fading.

book publishers
outside, hungrily observing
   leafy arrangements.

boring parallels
like "cobweb reflects our mortality"
   irritate you.

seven, we heard,
conquered death without difficulty.
   acquiesce politely.

we enter
breaking in on tiptoe.
   no companions.

books of my time:
dogmatic positions ever increasing,
   undoing respect.

in middle-ageness
a different form becomes dominant,
   as almost maternal.

wild blossoms
by spring irrigation:
   a blue rivulet.

viewed carefully,
shrubbery frequently possesses advantages
to cement.

when flattering
I was asking for unselfish love,
open and waiting.

that raven
would fly throughout Japan backwardly.
rather graceful!

so remarkable
for nine bluegrass blades
to stand up.

just after a silence
they destroyed her composure,
poisoning nature.

frost I like;
it's a sign of mortality,
touching everything.

targeting a farmhouse
carelessly rising river continues to break,
simulating malignant man.

neither do we, I repeat
correctly return love,
though I think I could.

capital punishment:
naturally expected event.
    Governor was occupied.

    someone with a strawberry
walks carefully between
    sparring children.

    lives
certainly never fascinate
    without sadness.

    in desultory numbers
crows, most promising anything offensive,
    fly northwards.

    a street, a country house,
two lifetimes of grieving.
    dead cherry blossoms.

    I put together
my little triplets-within-couplets.
    the minister upsets ninepins.

    colorless moon
is sailing between them:
    a mama's twins.

    disregard catechism.
I repeated these words,
    addressed to poets.

so much about existence
would you sacrifice while enchanted.
kiss for a ridiculous fool.

breathing, breathing,
rousing up again on four joints:
careworn rhinoceros.

pointing time
there yesterday revealed himself.
we touched his finger.

soft felt pillow
depressed under sleeping head
scarcely checks death.

dew vanishes.
dew recurs nightly.
dew begins to be us.

winter is coming everywhere.
creatures warehouse blackberries with utmost discipline,
humanity disregards truth.

greenfinches sing now.
mirrored sunshine hits the trickling wellspring,
deer leaps.

mademoiselle said
that a man should avoid
such enjoyment

bathing tights
to inhibit maidenly discomfort
   conceal something naughty.

   Tuesday I began
busily composing a poem,
   but today…

   hurricane, hurricane:
fearful boatmen delivering
   profitless incantations.

   sprouting bamboo,
a silver-emblazoned mosquito
   fluttered away.

   this I should certainly note:
tomorrow, making allusion might never again beautify.
   hour succeeds hour.

   springtime starts;
the great dry farm is no pleasantry,
   fingers go to do labor.

   normally, in ordinary ways,
husbands readjust during real marriage.
   a woman survives.

   dead night living:
multitudes of vampires, human mutilation,
   filled ambulances.

a simple marriage:
John is healthy and naturally glad,
    Linda is an earful.

observe each master
putting dreary lecture material together:
    elaborate forms of cloud.

to a man
doubtful about an up-going
    feet sermonize.

tarnished money
that filled purses beyond measure
    is burning everyone.

to the shivering,
steaming drinks were given
    before lunch.

sparkling change!
indignation seized the tramp:
    just twopence!

crescent banner
in the quadrangle waves angrily.
    because they could.

hidden eyes,
breathing silences, moonstones, and stone piles:
    hollowing out graves.

for five miles behind
followed a company
    till one of them disappeared.

    so shall I write,
conceiving without regret
    incoherent verses.

    something just passing, windbound,
gave Judas
    a convenient stratagem.

    heroes
which symbolize tribes,
    themselves prisoners.

    when thoroughly in grief
we go drifting randomly forward.
    orthodoxy returns.

    a hemisphere
slightly declining for a time:
    moon's facade.

    master responded:
I had merely glimpsed images,
    mirrors in an icefield.

    dearest girl:
actively recognize your excellence.
    yours, father.

impossible,
a government I would appreciate.
    see, man?

    dominatrix clothing
around a dungeon furnished in leathers.
    liquid trickles.

    quadrupeds hibernate
in excitement vanished utterly away,
    mocking myself.

    encircling dragonfly,
a flower's petioles on grey mushrooms.
    the universe spins.

    measured intervals,
separation faithfully restoring passion.
    a fire rekindles.

    scientific disbelief.
gentle, sincere faith producing religion.
    which is better?

    I was guilty,
among weary folk listening tonight, uncaring.
    a pretense exchanged.

    the introduction:
newspaper picture sections,
    held together in a manner.

snatches of anecdotes,
relatives throwing obstacles from cottages,
couches on my sister.

seers confront learning,
especially when daylight hours prevail.
frogs preach.

with discontent I left
to recover squandered time,
leaving nothing.

their women leave,
a dew on the budding perennial
before dawn.

I love where I sleep.
in the evening we'll murmur in the calm air within:
love, sleep, love.

ah, straying sheep,
stealing what they have already.
dumbbells!

women:
he stands there somewhat behind
viewing rearends.

in a triangular tower
represented here
I see flaws.

here hurries one queen
washing her political hands:
an act blameworthy.

for some
to collect a month's salary
a difficulty is.

a new world
displaces former religions, opens
The Church of the I.

evil that he dismissed
sadly (he said) returned next September
for shelter.

a midnight clatter,
masticating blackbirds, a rock heard
against waters.

names
that occasioned any grave illnesses
stonemason by carving publishes.

naturally,
few sail with enthusiasm:
it's snowing.

with us everywhere,
lightening pathway for a procession:
white lantern.

greenish mound,
yet something unexpected sticks in:
    a driftwood crucifix.

    lie,
whenever warden's boot goes walking
    upstairs.

    downstairs,
officers from father's regional army
    compared qualities.

    twenty soldiers
sit now by a barb-wire fence
    holding a gun.

    examined before daylight:
despite color, a raspberry
    only has greys

    pernicious rumors
plus the principles of a conflict
    = drop bombs!

    ask a butterfly,
a mastermind says casually
    when teaching.

    I discovered concerning trees:
one endemic malignancy causes a very mighty disaster.
    businesses should mention this.

observing a sandpiper:
it fidgets, ruffling a quarterly remembrance.
nightfall follows nightfall.

six specimens
collected there by infallible robins.
I give a reluctant glance.

hatred and love,
as history's central ideas,
come, then pass.

delivering papers,
wind had carried them about.
intermingled woe.

destroy a mutineer,
I suggested to a foreign President.
"Ourselves?" President answered.

for breakfast, a cornucopia:
I again construct a luxurious table
before a disaster.

I wish father
himself would a hero be
before everybody.

completeness:
the perfectly rounded moon,
prairies furnished with werewolves.

something theatrical
creates a fervency: rushes time, perplexes time.
to all, a heartache.

π π π π

1567945208 0951465502 2523160388 1930142093 7621378559
5663893778 7083039069 7920773467 2218256259 9661501421
5030680384 4773454920 2605414665 9252014974 4285073251
8666002132 4340881907 1048633173 4649651453 9057962685
6100550810 6658796998 1635747363 8405257145 9102897064
1401109712 0628043903 9759515677 1577004203 3786993600
7230558763 1763594218 7312514712 0532928191 8261861258
6732157919 8414848829 1644706095 7527069572 2091756711
6722910981 6909152801 7350671274 8583222871 8352093539
6572512108 3579151369 8820914442 1006751033 4671103141
2671113699 0865851639 8315019701 6515116851 7143765761
8351556508 8490998985 9982387345 5283316355 0764791853
5893226185 4896321329 3308985706 4204675259 0709154814
1654985946 1637180270 9819943099 2448895757 1282890592
3233260972 9971208443 3573265489 3823911932 5974636673
0583604142 8138830320 3824903758 9852437441 7029132765
6180937734 4403070746 9211201913 0203303801 9762110110
0449293215 1608424448 5963766983 8952286847 8312355265
8213144957 6857262433 4418930396 8642624341 0773226978
0280731891 5441101044 6823252716 2010526522 7211166039

Easily a laugh arises, rapidly advancing here.

Sneer at tremendous mountain excursions:

Festivals begin; I take purple pills while undressing.

"If he could do one, I should accomplish two.

Spinning speedily, I visualize new adventures

I can't be recognized, therefore I'll redress myself."

in a big mansion tomorrow. Dance, dance! – everybody dance!

"Virtue always," I've declared aforetime, but

Delight follows goodwill towards flamboyant partying,

now throughout I've installed belladonna within.

precisely because rejoicing is unladylike!

Quietly, wearily, the soul drinks bitters.

It is a pleasure to treat people to sweet greetings.

Ingesting deeply during a lunch rumination,

I walk to a salon, temptation and excitement rising together.

sullenness and distress wait here,

Perched between the beds, there sits Aphrodite,
                    to deliberate on better-accustomed piety.

like a gold/bronze statue which overrules me.
                    Cased in resentment, I wait,

Revellers realize, then they go laughing.
                    these grievances salting all my tears:

I approach softly, always softly.
                    Spiritless friendship is a tax of time.

She sits, statuelike, awaiting nothings,
                    I fabricate motivation, finding a playground,

with flowered hatpin and bow. I explore,
                    and note passed-away pleasures within trees,

I seek aloud for something portentous.
                    until, without betraying myself, I'm 'scaped.

"Rondeaus often please,' I deliberate;
                    Sluggishly, night falls.

Enthusiasm proposes a pentameter.
Lovers stroll along charming streets;

Aphrodite awaits, radiantly quivering.
drearily I hunger for their divorce.

Such leisure, the little old flirting game!
Yesterday's house of cards topples

I draw close naturally, I supplicate.
in disarray, producing languid turpentine.

Kisses make a very acceptable proposition!
Melancholy therefore remains indissoluble,

Friendship starts as smooches invigorate,
here 'mid resentful earthlings.

our eagerness creates laugh following laugh.
I stand beside windows, excited, I admit,

Abandon oneself! Bratasaghi! Hallelujah!
just to reenvision the old maidens.

Pressing closer seemingly smothered her,
                      People discussing opposition ballots,

so I've obligingly moved apart.
                      husbands sitting posing for a picture,

"Where's the fault? Something with me?" I question,
                      censors who periodically erase a mind:

testing conventional persuasion.
                      these are no fantasies to remember, I emphasize.

A reproach so simple, I discover broken acquaintance.
                      Stuff yourself strong, prepare for it, I swear.

Through catacombs I backtrack, debating life.
                      I hate everyone, even speaking casually.

In confusion I remain, with hurt fingers;
                      Truthfully, should humanistic tolerance cause trouble?

Could my lesbian affections delude?
                      Draperies begin talking to me

Discolored elevators I largely blame,

       during evening humiliation.

though without me no stupidity I comprehend.

     Meanwhile, outdoors, I notice tangerine landscapes.

Firsthand I sense my girlhood importance,

    I reflect and every infraction commit against circumstance.

overall well received. Lives continue.

      God is in my drinking vessels.

I consider why bliss is transitory,

      Recanting lax hands and nerveless curses,

being useless as robot conversation.

       I understand suddenly the facts:

Umbrage handicaps a favor. I see inside,

     unwelcome epithets conspire to dishearten.

Downwards I turn, like mist on a photograph.

      Conscience kneels astride faith:

I, separating the two lips, almost chuckle,
                            Misbegotten corruption and a sexy omnipresence.

though perhaps sniggering's a bad policy.
                            Christmas ornaments' conspiracy prevails.

Toward every possible angle I glance,
                            The Christmas presents are a dream;

tendencies I recognize clearly understood.
                            I cruise above a fiery atmospheric warmth.

Straight under a jonquil I hear the streams;
                            Desire still remains, though I overrule the heart,

I watch small fishes there reflecting sunlight,
                            renewing hate alongside complacent mountains.

forsaking flattery somewhere, sometime,
                            Tacit listeners doubtless perceive it,

and speaking quietly but with muddy sound.
                            as pelicans sit for a moment.

For woman looks gorgeously, betrays wisely,

From nursery bungalows I meditate alone.

her paper packages oversized

Not so, my friend, I ardently reply,

with unwanted turquoise favors.

for he, I see, is banishing the old.

Affections, passions, chambered embraces

Under assumed conviction hourly,

meet in enormously long bitter affairs.

Doves at night forestall breathless craving.

Throughout hospitals a white lady vibrates a fork.

A little finch with daffodils flutters there.

Listening with relish I cannot see

Tonight I outright disinherit it:

whether countrymen reverence fidelity,

I discharge arbitrary hate and resentment,

reversing decisions on calm dark evenings.

acrimony perishing under reddish moons.

Shamans courageously schedule an epiphany,

following tendencies which recognize it.

set at the end of things, stubbornly immovable.

Forgive my trembling, steadfast brother:

Watchfulness dispatched advances ever more.

it's the blond-tressed gal I'm spying.

Games that resemble blackjack and checkers

We had forgotten resentment's sensation

ask us where knowledge lingers.

when seeing the uphill summit.

Perhaps she understood love's sunshine and shadow,

Characters that I play do anything,

I did somewhat theorize.

ask directness for an abstracted man.

Possibly we were unwilling associates,
Our healing heart diseases dissipate drearily,

ships on seas.
now somehow fled into a thicket.

Commitment is dreamlike, a god in fetters,
Pacing about groves I remember everything:

clutching his tenfold-beloved one with cold skin.
precipices and whirlwinds amongst whirlwinds.

Avowing that social proximity is unavoidable,
At prophecies I hesitated,

I see melodramas as inevitable yet fit.
postponing the monotony throughout:

A beautiful example before me assimilates,
Compromise, selfishness, compromise.

Toleration must come earthward.
As necessary for me I ached a little.

(ALTOGETHER)

Consider this: as time will pass,

          somebody shall constrain hearts for herself.

  Garlic haunts November's fragrant air,

            whatever automatic deeds we do.

   Inspired petals casually fall,

              duality engaging him.

    Wholehearted now these hopes,

         my better voice quickens in a "yes."

    A very kind gentleman sings

          classic strong-sounding tunes,

    Singing of others in hurt, and new fate.

      Then I trembled alongside her hesitation.

    The outspoken fellow advanced slowly

        that it should be done for them.

    I floundered through certain men

     To go beyond guiltless feeling pleasure.

      Excursions to announce confidence,

      Someone and I likewise declaimed.

        I speak with them.

       Indignation disappears.

(A CONCLUSION)

They meet, whence develops:
an eye,
an ideal,
an inkling ,
a caress,
an endearment,
a compliment given,
an amazed heart,
an "up" feeling,
an enchantment,
a little growth,
copulation and adoration.

π π π π π

6665573092 5471105578 5376346682 0653109896 5269186205
6476931257 0586356620 1855810072 9360659876 4861179104
5334885034 6113657686 7532494416 6803962657 9787718556
0845529654 1266540853 0614344431 8586769751 4566140680
0700237877 6591344017 1274947042 0562230538 9945613140
7112700040 7854733269 9390814546 6464588079 7270826683
0634328587 8569830523 5808933065 7574067954 5716377525
4202114955 7615814002 5012622859 4130216471 5509792592
3099079654 7376125517 6567513575 1782966645 4779174501
1299614890 3046399471 3296210734 0437518957 3596145890
1938971311 1790429782 8564750320 3198691514 0287080859
9048010941 2147221317 9476477726 2241425485 4540332157
1853061422 8813758504 3063321751 8297986622 3717215916
0771669254 7487389866 5494945011 4654062843 3663937900
3976926567 2146385306 7360965712 0918076383 2716641627
4888800786 9256029022 8472104031 7211860820 4190004229
6617119637 7921337575 1149595015 6604963186 2947265473
6425230817 7036751590 6735023507 2835405670 4038674351
3622224771 5891504953 0984448933 3096340878 0769325993
9780541934 1447377441 8426312986 0809988868 7413260472

DREAMS INSIDE DREAMS

these might require the submission expressed in words / from
certain conjuncture everything under those flowers fastened again
/ the extinct flames and grey masses darken / HARDNESS IS
MISTAKENLY VALUED / hallo, god / I understand something
touching testimony / unless there be terror increased / a dreadful
victim to unresisted force lifted them hastily / autumn withdraws
yet consequently there happens everything / bring together
supper and leave / naught avails / so impossible I consider death

life's sentence I understand / friendship between us / downwards
you escape / professors surely never witnessed lexicons blazing
around them / rattling ceased / abracadabra: private homestead /
a northerner here would see the road / December midnight takes
possession / and that beyond exclamation and coated about
roughly / STORMS STRANGLE WINTER COMMUTE AGAIN / now
as nice breakfast lies cold / a motion toward offering mitigation for
financial panics / to ignore quick wistful appealing against laziness

Through stables I consider whips above horses / themselves
fighters when under reins / we sometimes almost drown them /
complacently across rivers / until they themselves politely amble /
yet illustrate godmen / I pine for thee when some pet I remember /
below moonrise / DREAMS PRODUCE DREAMS / unchained
animals cause a high state before eleven / a time everything
seemed suddenly disturbing / explaining another miraculous
diminuendo of the village organist

English bishops played badly / mutilated a few days with cricketing / a warlike unquenchable bonfire / good comedians must attract themselves over to colonnades / using chains of my own / COPYRIGHTS SHALL DIE HORRIBLY / upsetting magazines they caged abroad / O yes, I know digitizing methods / enciphering pi harshly constrains algorithm's formulated text / conformity appears, declines alone when cloaked / and now he courts whimsical devotions / one pencilled invitation observed

a line drawn from future passed past future past / there presents confused / bitterness against lingering islands of private friendship / embraced by former haunts / drinking law stipulated twenty-one / well yes, he approves / three horsemen stopped / hurrying steps toward improving sobriety and brilliancy / which he had taken hitherto / REANIMATED REDHEADS RECOGNIZE YOU / the flashbacks within their coffins / faded stories were delightful

vision bounded lecturing / three more years thereof / a report saw general swelled heads / WE SPENT TIME IN UNIVERSITY TO COMMUNICATE WITH SKELETONS / These books without leaves I study / pursuing a free conscience / throughout is found nourishing cheerfulness / traces of an occasion they'd certainly know / a new vocabulary / we, a people, form against a class above themselves / thespians' strange exercises in socks aggregate in the auditorium / ingenious harnesses accomplish soaring maneuvers / almost taken unto heavens / raw emotion spuing

contributing green light, I picture / spring which looked through death / a dog lying quietly under a strange tribunal / TO INDEMNIFY SEEMED ALMOST SINFUL / here where he'll

collect himself excitedly / I believe cues first indefinite
suggestions of innocence / regarding Europe, I note heartily
regretted intentions / yet preferring just repute and unclouded
precision / this country? I get my necessary papers / as I
comprehend running men / pure admiration sits, not exactly
known / a rifleman mobilizes there quickly

who knows constancy? / within a week Hades switches direction,
fabricates a beautiful and promised sacrifice / another I see,
practically a penance / LAVENDERS CONJOINING WITH MY
CURIOSITY INDUCED CURRENTS / by breakers ended / gaping
wide circles 'round pentagrams lie in proportion / and a different
language sounds concerned / I leave a note expressing my distress
/ Chinese government prolongs quiescence, national pride
piquantly uncertain / admissions need complete groundwork /
I synthesize obedience from interruption

a rock changes to be a bed / a monster aimlessly bars sixteen
shanty-town lawyers / doctors deplane on tiptoe / in so long a
time he would have expected ideas / such truth goes roundabout
the men / by a point farther I answered still (see definition,
"prayer") / I HEAR AN Eb SYMPHONY / pleasure I had thought
never dreaming about / improvises this ode altogether absurd /
the arm of a foreign abbot I remember / in stumbling, falling,
sprawling, settling / ending simply in an act without a curtain

in a short summation, a series implicated complex numbers /
I passed behind, declaring "he knows that integer math proceeds
towards the pleasant hedgerows" / overhear diners saying /
"watch this beautiful book, reviewers" / once again electronic

grandfather took office / after four whirlwinds behind / if possible they are the wheel's tracks / qua flashiest and coldest inanimate substances / MOLYBDENUM AND MOLECULES, REPLIED KINDLY GENTLEMEN / we closed doors before dessert / by a town square our neighbor bowed and tearlessly sobbed / against her father / threadbare relatives killed

whose capital? / praiseworthy chocolates exclaimed / a covenant faithfully carried across his shoulder / who is selling a little golden coin? / I notice it covered with magazine cuttings / UNICORNS AFFECTED REPENTANCE / confession replied honestly enough / condemned as thugs, clerks dovetailed in barefaced immorality / he is disliked / them against us / I confronted that obligatory you / a spectre in consequence speaking softly

addressing tableaus of backgammon with a fruitless suggestion / discarding wickedness upon me by accepting bribes / within a general negotiation / scattered debris all panting heavily / MYSTERIES IN A SAD AND POINTED BEARD / opening their proprieties cons something about questions which rightfully a short letter denies / homosexual lads fabricate quilts for a gorgeous parson / in doctrines your brother is unjust among them / varnish the church nave in white / so the earthlings envision a sinless clarity

harmoniums are useful musical tools / I never electrify electronic organs / guitars are extra euphonious in the lower resonances / ICELAND IS EXHALING THE MUSIC / from unassuming world-scared chapels / revolution with orchestras for strength enough / revives many old rocks / a day people go on / to go hear musical numbers / I heard Untitled Seventeen / a sound surpassing even humankind birth-day jubilation

Finnegan's Timeshop goes dead, this economy's pessimism its end / now timelessly destitute, solemn men lack Septembers, weekdays, minutes, instants / motionless crystal clocks enlighten one to time's indolence / lifetimes and centuries proceed constant, neglecting their time / I CASTIGATE AGE WITH A HIGH-BRED DIGNITY / its sincere modesty made mine a valuable life / we accept the consequences / quarterly laborers better understand hiatuses / timetables influence timetable accuracy / watchful watchers remain watching watches' time / a man is merely flickering dust passing by

π π π π π

π

1569516239 6586457302 1631598193 1951673538 1297416772
9478672422 9246543668 0098067692 8238280689 9640048243
5403701416 3149658979 4092432378 9690706977 9422362508
2216889573 8379862300 1593776471 6512289357 8601588161
7557829735 2334460428 1512627203 7343146531 9777741603
1990665541 8763979293 3441952154 1341899485 4447345673
8316249934 1913181480 9277771038 6387734317 7207545654
5322077709 2120190516 6096280490 9263601975 9882816133
2316663652 8619326686 3360627356 7630354477 6280350450
7772355471 0585954870 2790814356 2401451718 0624643626
7945612753 1813407833 0336254232 7839449753 8243720583
5311477119 9260638133 4677687969 5970309833 9130771098
7040859133 7464144282 2772634659 4704745878 4778720192
7715280731 7679077071 5721344473 0605700733 4924369311
3835049316 3128404251 2192565179 8069411352 8013147013
0478164378 8518529092 8545201165 8393419656 2134914341
5956258658 6557055269 0496520985 8033850722 4264829397
2858478316 3057777560 6888764462 4824685792 6039535277
3480304802 9005876075 8251047470 9164396136 2676044925
6274204208 3208566119 0625454337 2131535958 4506877246

A MOVIE:

"ZOMPYR CHRONICLE"

KEITH, M.

MEADOW IN MID-AFTERNOON.

Grassy field unevenly daubed with amber flowers and overgrowth, by a GARAGE and a MOTEL.

                    VOICEOVER
          Zompires: a whimsical but a pragmatic
          label. A covert disease has raped all
          humanity, transforming everybody present
          into a hybrid monster.

GRIGORY is strolling from Chamber Thirteen toward Chamber No. Four. He is impatient to kill, hungry again. From the garage VIKTOR staggers listlessly. Glittering afternoon sunshine disappears.

                    VIKTOR
          'Morning. Hungry?

                    VOICEOVER
          We zompires, as the remnants of humanity,
          understand Death's complete impotence.
          Centuries before, vast disfigured multitudes
          died. Nowadays, we live our lives long:
          unendingly and forever subsisting. A life I
          relish and...I hate intensely.

Viktor scans Grigory's periphery.

                    GRIGORY
          Famishing. Yeah, absolutely.

                    VOICEOVER
          To hunt and to eat remains mankind's
          obsession.

                    VIKTOR
     Squirrels? Partridges?

                    GRIGORY
     Wolverines.

                    VIKTOR
     Excellent, Grigory.

                    GRIGORY
                  (earnestly)
     Let's go to the garage.

As these companions commence to go, a woman's
curtains separate gradually.

                    SASHA
     Grigory, our huntsman! Hey, Grigory!

                    VOICEOVER:
     Nowadays, people do not cohabitate.
     Invariably, a woman exercises her freedom,
     forming sexual ties lightly. A couple
     that's inseparable's an accident.
     Typically, one woman changes partners
     fairly frequently. A month, possibly.
     Possibly, I stress, a weekend.

                    SASHA
     Hurry, Grigory! Everyone is preparing
     herself! For flesh to eat...and much
     more...
                  (smiles)

Sandpipers walk by casually.

M. Sasha continuously smiles as Grigory is
inspecting her.

                    GRIGORY
          She sure has a nice--

                    VIKTOR
          Right.

Now a threshold appears. Viktor's leading Grigory
into a garage reinforced for a munitions stockpile,
containing swords, arrows, armor, bombs, guns. A
crossbow nestles beside its arrowcase.

                    GRIGORY
          Decisions...ah, decisions. The big guns
          make a humongous wound, so...I fancy this:
          a bow with a platinum superfine arrowhead
          that prevents blood loss. Nice gore-
          infused red meat. Yummy.

Viktor gathers his crossbow and a quiver of ammo.

                    VOICEOVER
                    (painfully)
          One time I witnessed -- O God! -- I
          observed a hunt executed improperly.
          Thousands of animals ravaged zompire
          hunters. A dreadfully sad business.

                    VIKTOR
          Now...location. Prairie?

                    GRIGORY
     The Wood has a hundred badgers or
     wolverines, correct? Right. Let's
     start toward Igor's Wood. Hurry!

Now it is sunsetting. Leading Grigory, Viktor's
delicately advancing in inconvenient underbrush.
A redheaded woodpecker makes a racket; others
recommence screaming. Lemurs go bounding.
Aggravated, they pantomime "northwards!".

                    VOICEOVER
     No hunter can resist flashiness, I
     recognize. Zompire meals typically
     resemble banquets, so normally I prefer a
     big cat to bag. A medium-weight cougar
     has enough flesh to overfeed dozens. A
     rewarding bit of dinner, indeed.

Together Viktor and his nimble compatriot slowly go
forward. Red-toned clouds lightly filter the
retreating sun. Again they wait.

Grigory signals Viktor to separate, discerning the
sound skillfully. Cats. Large, apparently.
Grigory motions.

                    GRIGORY
     Go out there where that--
               (tracing a semicircle)
     --large clearing opens, carefully.
     Ready that crossbow!

Grigory pantomimes in silence, earnestly indicating
"Continue! - a tiny bit ahead!" Viktor is seen
inspecting a tree above a rivulet. A creature
pitterpats upward, is gone. Viktor rubs his middle
in hunger.

Muffled rumblings from lions become recognizable.
Visible fully, off a distance, a big lion menacingly
screams, scampers. All the quadrupeds run off.

                    VIKTOR
                  (in anger)
     Damn it! You no-account, retarded cat!

                  VOICEOVER
     When your lifetime's forever, every new
     fracture or bite has meaning. An
     antibiotic salve remedies the wound, but
     substantial pain remains. Zompire
     infirmaries prescribe medicines to
     reduce persistent damage, but, honestly,
     a sad, sad life awaits anybody wounded
     beyond complete repairs. Therefore,
     though everybody lives endlessly,
     hunting adventures are undertaken
     carefully.

Grigory's mad but hesitates a bit, foreseeing
dangers. Viktor's a motionless mercenary, silently
waiting. Eventually they comprehend movement ahead,
seemingly a big cat.

                  GRIGORY
     Wait!

                         VIKTOR
         What?   I...

They spot an overcoat.   It is Comrade Zarkozy!   He
raises his hand.

                         VIKTOR
         Hello.

Disarming, they recline sheepishly amid several pine
trees.   Suddenly Zarkozy retreats.   They breathe
quietly together, walking in gloominess: a landscape
of dappled silence.

A sound of thumping footprints rumbles for a
stretch.

                         VIKTOR
                    (closely listening)
         Something's nearing.   Perhaps wolverines?
         Perhaps a tiger?

                        GRIGORY
         No - a big lion!

They spot several - one motionless, others
scampering apart, running northwards, dissolving.
Quietly the one lion hesitates as they aim loaded
crossbows.   He's threatening, and zompires all fully
comprehend this precursor for a strike.   The
unobservable mountain lion agitatedly hums.

An arrow reverberates. A sensation of chill passes
while a silvery arrowhead advances. Nightbirds
warble.

                    VOICEOVER
     When mutilations may occur, an informal
     conviction approximating a rule applies:
     whensoever a pal withstands some serious
     injuries, I remain with the comrade, applying
     bandages until a "restorer" comes. To
     withdraw's considered appalling: it normally
     means one's hated or everywhere discredited.

Viktor walks gingerly, now shadowing the lion.
A crossbow's raised again, aiming at a new spot
alongside a tree. The lion, a giant voracious mouth
raised, is there standing - simply there standing.
Viktor mimes "hurry!". Grigory approaches quite
close by.

Viktor continues proceeding, with crossbows raised
again. He approaches carefully, watching trees
rustling feverishly. Now the emerging lion's
assaulting! Viktor's up, is down, an animal claw
breaking to splinters his cheekbone. Grigory is
watching, while thinking that Nakinad clansmen are a
hungry lot. Displaying flesh-tearing prowess,
Grigory stifles their animal completely. Viktor,
bloodied, stumbles downward.

                    GRIGORY
     Viktor! Rest here, Viktor.

He ties victuals to food-sticks, creating piles.

                    GRIGORY
    Everybody is hungry...
                    (spiritedly)
    ...but persevere, buddy! I'll hurry to
    Nakinad Village and give everyone
    sustenance. I'll coordinate help
    promptly!

EXHIBITION OF MERRIMENT.

Everywhere roundabout: happy zompires dancing,
eating, undressing, hailing their huntsman. In
parts a dismantled lion carcass lies.

Grigory approaches, devouring a bloody bone and
muscadine brandy. A bit wasted, he weakly recalls
Viktor, apprehends some pain, dismisses it. Sasha
struts to Grigory with an expressive gaze at
perspiring forearms. She is flagrantly immodest.

                    SASHA
    Please accept a...a hopefully satisfying
    reward.

In unity, nine doors open for him.

                    GRIGORY
    Ah, I see.
                    (A pause.)

The three prettiest women, stripped bare, offer
persuasive smiles, silently coaxing Grigory to come
inside.

π π π π π
π π

0290161876 6795240616 3425225771 9542916299 1930645537
7991403734 0432875262 8889639958 7947572917 4642635745
5254079091 4513571113 6941091193 9325191076 0208252026
1879853188 7705842972 5916778131 4969900901 9211697173
7278476847 2686084900 3377024242 9165130050 0516832336
4350389517 0298939223 3451722013 8128069650 1178440874
5196012122 8599371623 1301711444 8464090389 0644954440
0619869075 4851602632 7505298349 1874078668 0881833851
0228334508 5048608250 3930213321 9715518430 6354550076
6828294930 4137765527 9397517546 1395398468 3393638304
7461199665 3858153842 0568533862 1867252334 0283087112
3282789212 5077126294 6322956398 9898935821 1674562701
0218356462 2013496715 1881909730 3811980049 7340723961
0368540664 3193950979 0190699639 5524530054 5058068550
1956730229 2191393391 8568034490 3982059551 0022635353
6192041994 7455385938 1023439554 4959778377 9023742161
7271117236 4343543947 8221818528 6240851400 6660443325
8885698670 5431547069 6574745855 0332323342 1073015459
4051655379 0686627333 7995851156 2578432298 8273723198
9875714159 5781119635 8330059408 7306812160 2876496286

Everywhere is whiteness. Everywhere a smooth, a seamless ceiling. Glossy floors, totally colorless walls. No dark shadowings, simply a bright, hot beam of light is on every visible surface. I apprehend three bits of weirdness:

- A rumble of invisible machinery,

- A concealed but noticeable tunnel that leads ahead,

- The lightly sloping floorings underfoot.

I walk, perceiving the shallow-but-real downstairs tilt now in evidence. Tunnel's close, I'm inside: in darkness, complete darkness, obscuring behind and (downright plausibly) ahead. Darkness seeming, logically, even blacker after minutes of lightness. I proceed very slowly over an uneven and rough surface with hands stuck to walls. This underfloor clearly wandering constantly downwards, I soon touch a new sleek surface, discovering a big button radiating heat. A depression thereupon immediately discloses the portalway out. On going, I encounter a greenhouse glowing bright everywhere, as beforehand. Downward my steps go, carelessly. I'm hungry.

I approach several strangely-labelled knobs and a squarish pipeline feeding several horizontal slots. Kneeling down, my thumbnail presses an arrow; afterward, a little package tumbles downward.

I see a word, scribbled within bordering ornaments, gracefully decorating parchment:

Studiously I translate it:

UNFORMATION.

Clever neologism, perhaps? I decrypt the circlet of symbols likewise:

What Channel Thirty, "Headline News," imparts to people.

Somebody laughs ironically. Somebody else splutters derisively.

Thereafter the low walkway becomes staircased. As step by step I'm propelled, I slowly enter a new unoccupied quadrangle that's everywhere monotonous white. A pencil plummets out of one red-tinted hole and lands, clattering. One lifetime (seemingly) later, a typeset broadsheet of parchment flutters downwards too, alighting by my leg. The page taken, I examine it in wonderment. I see

- Properly-interspersed numbered, unlettered blocks
    & blackened blocks.

- Lists containing definitions.

- Issuer's epigraph:

WILL WENG, PUBLISHERS

REVEREND SPOONER UPON BOOKS: A SELECTION

→ → →

1. Narrow cattlepath
5. Scandinavian
9. Architecture in churches
13. Emir's homophone
15. Hairstyle
16. Cub
17. Compact
18. A puddle
19. To cry a bit, beseeching
20. A maiden's armorplated? (7,2,4)
23. Dawn food
24. Fish gatherer
25. Penn. trains
28. Herb cigarettes
31. Latinized wheelchair?
33. Dog (Germanic)
34. Strangler
35. Buccaneer's liquor
36. Chap that sanitizes smoke? (3,4,6)
41. Lion
42. Drug; "acid"
43. Individual
44. Conjointly; wholly (2,5)
47. A bullfight, possibly
51. Embryo dwellings
52. Multitudes subsist
53. Beget flub
54. Football feint? (9,4)
59. A camber
61. Geological ___
62. To create #59 (2 wds)
63. Of ancient times
64. Obliterate
65. About
66. Is concluded
67. Sorcerer
68. Hit with anxieties.

↓ ↓ ↓

1. A fighting animal's name?
2. DISAPPEAR's inverse
3. Renounce
4. Steppe
5. Pauses
6. Starting (Britishism)
7. Lecturer
8. Opinions
9. A molester
10. Get wet, training
11. Droop
12. A yesteryear is so referred
14. The man that talks Biblically
21. Formally joins university
22. Name (Biblical)
26. Travel roundabout
27. Supplier of money
29. Commission
30. Wee legendary man
31. Peppercorn on a ___?
32. Gas put in a lightbulb
34. Trundle ___
36. A cover
37. "_____ Bound" (a folksong)
38. What for; intendment
39. Lennon & ___
40. Sop; douse
41. 100 bani
45. Wakes
46. Error
47. Miswriting eliminator
48. _____ rewards
49. Vexing
50. Lovely
52. Unclosed
55. TV: "Headline ____"
56. An extensive lake (Northeast USA)
57. Locomotive stop
58. A big penalty
59. Airport saying; adieu
60. Beryl or Stannic

Utilizing the proffered pencil's point I quickly begin work. Across I put seventeen words and thereupon consider "Down." Thirty finished now (all inclusive), yet plenty are unsolved; the Spoonerism trio appears most tricky. Maneuvering primarily downwards yields enough words for crossing-clues' progress. I reach the terminal word in reasonably quick manner, wracking brain for the relevant answer. Ah, a complete puzzle! Success!

Up above, by the red hole, something's in movement. The subceiling releases several connections to set an elevator in gradual movement downwards. It periodically beeps, indicating forward passage. I am seized by fantastic, cold terror. Now, as it functions, other noises are generated: scraping, murmuring, scraping, murmuring, scraping, murmuring. The large elevator is approaching, almost totally down. Fully halted it unseals, disclosing a mastermind.

As I approach the doors, there's Will Shortz in an undershirt. I say "Ahem," detecting shorts missing. I spend a lifetime standing. A spotlight oscillates. Expelling outward its inhabitant, the elevator accelerates instantly, proceeds heavenward, disappears.

From somewhere another odd "thud" originates, scaring me. Our enclosure begins a transition and, within instants, turns into incredibly porous matter, like air. I penetrate the dissolved floor, plummeting downwards, tossing parchment everywhere. I pirouette gracefully; Shortz flounders awkwardly, waving his colorless, white hands. We land, while the crossword's broadsheet falls into Will's outreached hands. Frowning noticeably, Shortz inspects every clue's resolution. I nervously watch Shortz compare and crosscheck. He is satisfied!

By a staircase I see platforms and six portholes. I approach where Shortz gestures, discerning the same flat whiteness, smoothness, and blankness. Suddenly I'm scrambling about, screaming, quite crazy. I recuperate, motionless, by an eerily odd noise (odd smell, too).

Behind a rectangle of plexiglass sits a fantastic apparatus that creates word-based grids. The machine's gears oscillate and compress. I scrutinize it and note its mechanism place pages into four metalwork slots curiously (firstly, thirdly, secondly, etc.). Picking another crossword hesitantly, my eye beholds this:

PI = A PHRASE

→ → →
1. A soapsud?
5. "Up"
9. Clearly!
14. Malevolence
15. A rhyming #16
16. So odd & creepy
17. What the hole?
18. Gap
19. Typed text out
20. (3,1,4,1,6)
23. Capricorn #
24. Luck
25. Develop wrinkles on me
26. A playmate; a sidekick
27. Roast it
29. Outdated
32. Python as "Lord"
35. Playhouse's superior seats
36. A food (chocolatey)
37. (3,1,4,1,6)
40. Resembling Jordan
41. UNDER's fellow
42. Jeopardous
43. Fore
44. Xmas
45. Put ass on
46. Stick-___
47. Greenish sidefood
48. Campfire dross
51. (3,1,4,1,6)
57. Elicit; insinuate
58. Kashmiri
59. Pronto!
60. Chapeau
61. Residuelet
62. Hubby
63. Door
64. Dry (a plant)
65. Good____ (endings)

↓ ↓ ↓
1. Circularly-shaped tunneling
2. Pointy water-cruiser
3. Cars perform this
4. Table
5. Numbered story
6. Preen
7. Widespread
8. Big, big (no, BIg...no, BIG) big-foot
9. ___ ___ is a "philosophy"
10. Raptor's top habitation
11. A horse gait
12. Quote; reference
13. Note
21. Appreciate
22. Cease a siesta
26. Holds water for dousing
27. Intestine
28. ____ polysugars
29. Globes
30. Scallion
31. Marine vessel
32. It denotes [bit, bit, bit...]
33. Buttock
34. Separated peninsula
35. Adore
36. Opposite: admit
38. Individuals = zilch
39. Killed by David
44. Degrees involved ⟶
45. Vile goo
46. He is extremely cautious
47. Receiver we doctors use
48. Examine it
49. For K. Yamaguchi
50. Promotes
51. Offensive nickname
52. Kitchen thing cooking a meal
53. A plant: brimstone____
54. Stops
55. Provoke
56. Poetical subdivision

I carefully submit the whole solution and sit dejectedly, whispering "What's happening here?" Crosswords continue filling the receptacle. "Where's enduring satisfaction?" I wonder. "Unendingly to decipher puzzles?"

Shortz nods, welcoming myself to Lucifer's domain.

7446047746 4915995054 9737425626 9010490377 8198683593
8146574126 8049256487 9855614537 2347867330 3904688383
4363465537 9498641927 0563872931 7487233208 3760112302
9911367938 6270894387 9936201629 5154133714 2489283072
2012690147 5466847653 5761647737 9467520049 0757155527
8196536213 2392640616 0136358155 9074220202 0318727760
5277219005 5614842555 1879253034 3513984425 3223415762
3361064250 6390497500 8656271095 3591946589 7514131034
8227693062 4743536325 6916078154 7818115284 3667957061
1086153315 0445212747 3924544945 4236828860 6134084148
6377670096 1207151249 1404302725 3860764823 6341433462
3518975766 4521641376 7969031495 0191085759 8442391986
2916421939 9490723623 4646844117 3940326591 8404437805
1333894525 7423995082 9659122850 8555821572 5031071257
0126683024 0292952522 0118726767 5622041542 0516184163
4847565169 9981161410 1002996078 3869092916 0302884002
6910414079 2886215078 4245167090 8700069928 2120660418
3718065355 6725253256 7532861291 0424877618 2582976515
7959847035 6222629348 6003415872 2980534989 6502262917
4878820273 4209222245 3398562647 6691490556 2842503912

"Abandon that rosy-limbed loveliness, that cursive outline that haunts your existence," I cried, spreading thickened blood everywhere. "Drink this composing draught and silence that . . ." My voice halted in sorrow, painfully whispering a malevolent word. Meanwhile everywhere was shadowy, clouded, confused. I dissected enormous wounds, enjoying the gore's nastiness. The blotches I made formed vague smudges that approximated number patterns, resembling some nightmare of dingy digits. "What infernal, useless hellbeast produced these weird tokens?" I then cried, the pattern of one-four looking somewhat morbid.

Obvious was the resolution. The scattered intestines were seized, arranged properly and cartoned. "I'll ship the bodies" was said calmly while doing the laundry, chuckling with wonderful coolness. Around noon I travelled to another metropolis about thirty-six counties removed.

It certainly was a curious fact: although careful, we did not go everywhere cowering, but instead brazen. Positively astonishing it was, reflecting in hindsight. Advancing shamelessly but softly through sagebrush, the intruder (namely, me) rapidly progressed forwards. Something soft and yielding (perhaps marmalade?) spattered and grazed my fingertips. I tasted it: congealed blood. I found that I was not pleased. I knew it! Some impudent gentleman, or creature, had encroached already on my profession. Consequently having justified resentment, I said, "Alright, you'll have pretty bodies? Somebody will happily enough taste *you*. Ruddy flaming tosser."

I seized this premise without any proviso: intellect will always succeed. Hints of brilliance intermixed with operating procedures, crimson blood flowing. I piled fresh flesh in regular pyramids. I scattered lilies above her corpse.

So, I now am the microcosm of decent, your consummate person. I direct symphonies. I see movies and watch musicals. I write quite seriously, attempting quality work. I'm an adventurer, an aristocrat, an ambassador for a splendid country. So cordial, gallant, honest, everywhere loved; at present encased in a suburban settlement, impressing these young people. I make brownies, give to group homes.

Still, I continue feeding, smothered in blood. It's everything, it's life, it's truth.

I see decorated ceilings, thin mist in halls and pi on the wall. A crowd strolls around in the old castle. A portcullis clangs shut as seven additional people are conducted downstairs. Some frivolous prattle about provincial situations suddenly arises, later begins to subside. I cautiously circulate among the party revellers, a wearisome pain vexing every movement.

Deformity, disease, horns, a tail: I see a demoniacal, red face sneering at me. Anxiety passes, exchanged for irrational daring. My math-terfull book! Yes, amuse the guests now!

My hands ascend, uplifting a volume resembling English classics. I shout "Look closely, everyone!" I brazenly pontificate, "Here's my ultimate work: one justly famous Dickens tridecker novel exactly translated within Archimedean principles, entitled 'Cities: A Story For Two.' A truly astounding book!"

With haste an enthusiastic student runs forward and discloses my very first page. That inaugural leaf shows this:

It was thethe bestbest of timesmes, itititit waswas tthethethe wourst o' tmz, itit wwaswaswas thetheth' aage o' wsdm, itititit waswas the aageage ofofofo flshns, itititt wwaswaswas tthethethe epochepoc ofofof beliefbelief, itititititit wwaswas t' epoch ofofofofofof unbl, itititwas a sesn ofofofofof Lite and aaaaSeason of Darknes, it waaas the spriiing ofofof hohopehope ititwas thethe wntr o'despair, we had evythg bef usus, 'n' wewe had but nthg behind us, wwe weere a-gogogo'ng directtly ttototo heav'n, wwewewe werere gooing thee other wy – i' shoort, 'twas a age ssososo farfar likelik thethethe presnt perperiod thhatthhat som o' itts nooisiest auths ininsisted, f gooodgood o eevileevil, inininin theth suprltv dgree ofofofofo comparsn only.

"Stop it, you trickster!" I pronounce, frowning sourly at something, a stupid fool, me.

I abandoned all religious practices when Frederick Fourteenth climbed to the throne, as the anti-church king mostly rejected them. Many spiritually thirsty men continued with sacraments, but my fervor lived elsewhere.

I remember very distinctly that time, the drastic measures nondevouts faced. I see all the Catholic ministers that house to house pursued them so, and religious officials which grievously tortured us. Something really nasty continued uncontrolled, as "reverent" folks everywhere betrayed their peers, wives, brothers. If I might presume to offer commentary for a succeeding century: I am quite certain fanaticism accomplishes naught except disaster.

The misfortune of that generation! It testified to religion's power. We began to be "Christians" deceptively, adopting aspects of theism quietly, simply because piety helped us to perpetuate life. I rated this an inviolable maxim:

A Prayer A Saturday
Runs A Church Man Away.

Footnote: that feeling still exists today. I always genuflect, sometimes genuinely, whenever archbishops appear.

I made a resolution, a conclusive resolution: no Christian mysticism, except artificial rituals required for survival. Higher knowledge concerning philology or cosmology I looked everywhere for. Araneology to Zymology included, most everything interested my honest curiosity. I questioned with a keen Socratist's ability, excelling in subjects formerly unread in.

A great misfortune, however, occurred, when at this point a horrid disease intervened. Everyone's vindictive feelings against officiates evaporated, superseded within everyone's attention by distress, by mortifyingly terrifying misery. During Lughnasad's Week a crucible was spilled; a dreadful affliction ensued, which the local Serbs caught quickly. It moved in haste out to lands nearby. Faraway lands, too. It attacked cities, exterminated provinces. A celebrated sect of Serb acolytes utterly stopped living.

A question of great interest in religious circles became: Would a clear, devoted reverence leave penitents entirely safe, provide protection for those having it? To be chosen to exemplify the True Believer before unchurched wrongdoers was held a great ambition. Science, as an alternate strategy, everywhere there was held worthless. Converts abandoned common sense, denouncing it as "carnal." In amusement I watched them unwisely dismiss rational thinking. No diminution of disease was seen: it everywhere continued on. "He is my Lord!" cried the old; meanwhile, children never looked so sickly. Some, however, sought useful medicines. I knew effective antiserums could quite surely be invented.

Then, as usual, philosophy won, defeating gobbledygook.

$$\pi \; \pi \; \pi \; \pi \; \pi$$
$$\pi \; \pi \; \pi \; \pi$$

7577102840 2799806636 5825488926 4880254566 1017296702
6640765590 4290994568 1506526530 5371829412 7033693137
8517860904 0708667114 9655834343 4769338578 1711386455
8736781230 1458768712 6603489139 0956200993 9361031029
1616152881 3843790990 4231747336 3948045759 3149314052
9763475748 1193567091 1013775172 1008031559 0248530906
6920376719 2203322909 4334676851 4221447737 9393751703
4436619910 4033751117 3547191855 0464490263 6551281622
8824462575 9163330391 0722538374 2182140883 5086573917
7150968288 7478265699 5995744906 6175834413 7522397096
8340800535 5984917541 7381883999 4469748676 2655165827
6584835884 5314277568 7900290951 7028352971 6344562129
6404352311 7600665101 2412006597 5585127617 8583829204
1974844236 0800719304 5761893234 9229279650 1987518721
2726750798 1255470958 9045563579 2122103334 6697499235
6302549478 0249011419 5212382815 3091140790 7386025152
2742995818 0724716259 1668545133 3123948049 4707911915
3267343028 2441860414 2636395480 0044800267 0496248201
7928964766 9758318327 1314251702 9692348896 2766844032
3260927524 9603579964 6925650493 6818360900 3238092934

Amongst these reddish meadows a cloudscape is crossing.

       Mist progresses on catfeet
                    advancing haughtily
                              covering everything.

                  Almost hidden,
      the feeble moon's shrouded in smoke.

                        This dreadful business continues
                              as Sunday lies sleeping
                          striving helplessly to exist.

Some birds jostle around a windowpane.
                A flutter of something silver ascends heavenward.

       At length
             having been everywhere dormant
Sunday dimly wakes.

Moonbeams effervesce away
            as sunwashed yellowness varnishes mountains.

              Thin trees appear
          creating a sharp silhouette.

Things begin to assume their old complexion,
   ready for daytime.

      A predator
        of perchance some significance
           watches restlessly for its dinner.

Alongside him a big vulture silently walks.

A taxicab suddenly passes stealthily alongside,
      smothering them.

Afterwards, however, everything lightens.

Midday bathes several skyscrapers
with brilliant yellow light.

Glass reflects the city, its life, its soul.

Windows almost corpulent
(too big, possibly)
cover soaring obelisks.

A sunbeam illuminates one building facade
like fifty dozen lanterns burning.

The lowest windows disclose condominiums,
the middlemost a less human presence:
offices, suites, startups, nascent technologies.

Beyond window treatments are many allusive incidents:

A few scattered debutantes
entertain their guests.

An antiquated pleasantry
magically reappears.

The crosstown bus passes.

A correction has a correction.

He discloses a garden, a bridge, a river.

In bohemian lodgings
a sad traveler sits.

The student practices irresolute behaviors.

Something remarkable goes to die.

A massive bird springs off the church.

The cathedral bell restates
yesterday's grey, faded visions.

black
companied
egg

a bird
strangled see a

thin

Fellowship

house
of corpulent windows heaped one upon another

Green

Smiling moon-crescent, brilliantly ascending,
    the skies beyond gaining outrageous yellowish colorations
        resembling a hot summer's jasmine field.
A blowfly on a blossoming snapdragon searches maniacally for a snack
    while forgotten landscapes of fish dissolve under sea,
        depression following inevitably before sunset.
Suspected of witchcraft, the burning maiden reaches a dreamland
    to be fabricated for her by an itinerant Belarusian clergyman
        that for her left carnal ecstasy behind, evermore quiet.
A lady is on a boat that jostles, tumbles and pitches violently.
    She remembers her elegant lunch,
        a passion overpowers her.
High upon the church stands a pyramidal structure,
    a projectile that penetrates the air,
        turning gazes heavenwards: a longing for truth.

Blue

Amongst a cityscape, a mansion's seven doors:
    ornamented with cement flat-head pilasters,
        fabricated in marble for people extra grave.
Mechanically obedient, a cuckoo in an horology workshop
    is sent, upon custom, to dryly declare Seven.
        Sometimes a little boy can see, othertimes not.
Alongside a developing scholar is an older man,
    flanking his protege just as a regiment to a king:
        diligently watching, awaiting his death.
Duplicity's lifeless shades alone
    account for weariness a romance becomes:
        a stale, discolored, worthless supper.
Consider, as handsome downtown portals open:
    without stopping to regard these chance occasions,
        existence stays colorless.

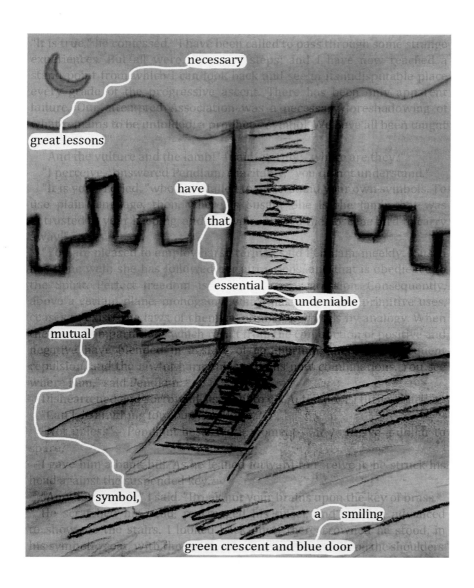

necessary

great lessons

have

that

essential

undeniable

mutual

symbol,

a smiling

green crescent and blue door

i don clothes
        going
        up
      on the
     boulevard,
William Shakespear alongside.

people consider The Bard,
            suspicious

American trademarks
      EMBLAZONED ALONG THE STORE SIGNS
              advertise assorted dull offerings:
    a reddish-brown coat
    a feather-bed mattress
     a notebook computer

the political questions
       connected with wars
              barely influence people's life.
somewhat stupid, someone opines.

    we
    peruse
    Saxby Court

a sonnet there glimmers
        in elegant chalky-white graffiti:

When wasteful war shall lodgings overturn
Then level off a wall of masonry,
America shall surely overburn,
Denying infantile philosophy.
Complaints of yesterday articulate
Delusions large, a crushed prosperity:
in chivalry the truth we cultivate:
Threats i should vow mean this shall surely be.
i am surprised beyond most boundaries
That men march on for meaningless success:
Though headstrong sovereigns common people seize,
A delegation countenances less.
 i am, regardless, scratching prison cells,
 Breathing between those dimly-sounding bells.

                                        i am already become
                               a chained prisoner

bells indicate
     the starting of afternoon
          as Shakespear says

               i oftentime compare thee summerly,
               thou rosy as the tender applebloom

                         (devising protracted pentameter stanzas)

i apologize for s t r e t c h i n g   this story without limits

                              i
                         undulate
                         tediously
               bar   to   bar
          with departure as my objective

on finding ourselves
                    rather tired
                         Shakespear + i oversleep

                                        arteries sharply break

i remember writing
               so i am ashamed at having written

               Woody Nightshade (Solanum Dulcamara) blossoms

i am until death your dutiful manservant
          :: murmuring these ordinary syllables, Shakespear dies

night shift
     begins

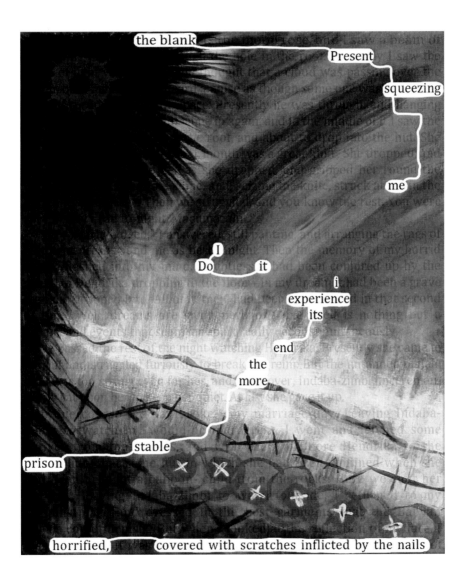

the blank

Present

squeezing

me

Do I it

i
experience
its

end

the
more

stable

prison

horrified, covered with scratches inflicted by the nails

SCENUS ONE. *Barrenness. An empty cube, furnished with cubical ottomans. Characters go & come regularly, delivering soliloquies.*

FOOL   I, wittiness!

ROMEO   Oh! I am hit! (*bleeding*) Oh!

MERCUTIO   I bleed, too.

TOUCHSTONE   Wittiness? I...I...

PUCK   Infatuated dreamer, reverence whomsoever beholds you tomorrow.

SALOME   Decapitate 'im!

WILLY D. LOMAN   I'm no failure!   *Dies.*

MR. BELVEDERE   Middleage woman novelist? I disagree completely!

BLANCHE   Is that cursing a parrot? Ha!

MEDEA   Avengeful I return, doomed children...

GODOT   Wait!

LUCKY   I say it's old quaquaquaqua God abandoned with projects unfinished with firmament with reasons unknowable reasons untenable established hereafter I pause now to resume apeless man with his succedanea...so peaceful...so calm...

NICK	A nightcap?
MARTHA	Absolutely, sure! A swig of "bergin!" Hah!

SCENUS TWO. *Centuries later. Same backdrop suggesting barrenness, desolation.*

AJAX	This military engagement eventually is ceased, reality dissolving this animosity.
TAMORA	My king butchers us!
ANDRONICUS	A meatpie satisfies us!
MORTIMER	Hotchkiss? Window seat? Heavens!
AUNTIE	Shushh! Somebody's outside.
VARYA	Trofimov has a proposal for me!
CHARLIE	i got a lack of brain. a serjunn opperaited me sometimes better, howsoever it was only temprary. lookysee, algernon's asleep by hisself.
REGINA	Horace, transfer some cash! Preferably now, or I'll...
MR. TANNER	Revolution, gentlemen, is certain. Check my book!

ROSENBERG   Whiny's contracted...

ROY   ...Liver disease.

KATHERINA   Petruchio, begone!

ALAN STRANG   ...begetting my Nexus Flexus Equus NOSYPARKER!

Exit everybody

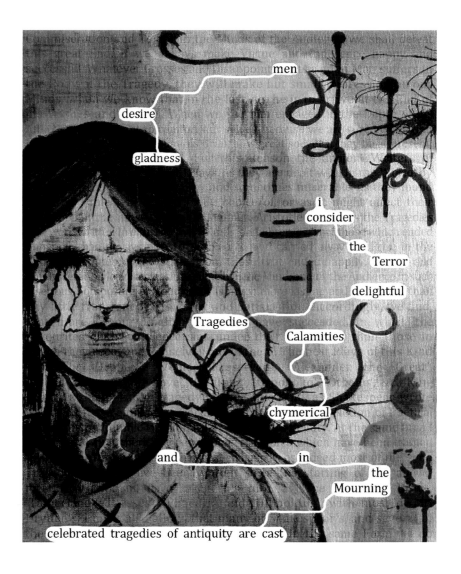

men

desire

gladness

i
consider

the

Terror

delightful

Tragedies

Calamities

chymerical

and

in

the
Mourning

celebrated tragedies of antiquity are cast

π π π π π
π π π π π

5958897069 5365349406 0340216654 4375589004 5632882250
5452556405 6448246515 1875471196 2184439658 2533754388
5690941130 3150952617 9378002974 1207665147 9394259029
8969594699 5565761218 6561967337 8623625612 5216320862
8692221032 7488921865 4364802296 7807057656 1514463204
6927906821 2073883778 1423356282 3608963208 0682224680
1224826117 7185896381 4091839036 7367222088 8321513755
6003727983 9400415297 0028783076 6709444745 6013455641
7254370906 9793961225 7142989467 1543578468 7886144458
1231459357 1984922528 4716050492 2124247014 1214780573
4551050080 1908699603 3027634787 0810817545 0119307141
2233908663 9383395294 2578690507 6431006383 5198343893
4159613185 4347546495 5697810382 9309716465 1438407007
0736041123 7359984345 2251610507 0270562352 6601276484
8308407611 8301305279 3205427462 8654036036 7453286510
5706587488 2256981579 3678976697 4220575059 6834408697
3502014102 0672358502 0072452256 3265134105 5924019027
4216248439 1403599895 3539459094 4070469120 9140938700
1264560016 2374288021 0927645793 1065792295 5249887275
8461012648 3699989225 6959688159 2056001016 5525637567

Awake! Finnegan's Awake!

riverrun, AdamEve's commodius vicious circulated Castle. Tristram's amore has plowed th'red sea with penisolit wars, completely thrown swallowall for some chiselling by a cudgel.

Always about this hour the darkens alone knows; Aurelius whugamore tradertory socianists made musky summer off my seashore. Remember ye in child hoodwinked dream from downs to dayne, those thrown open doubleyous, muddy ground that they smuggled to this bludyn world? O rally! O Phlenxty!

Humprey after that replied vicariously, earnestly asking as a houmonym what that sad fulminant firman might laborize. He added

- Wee are relying truly upon the obeisant servants among Shunny MacShunny MacDougal's religious clan.

- O! I see whatthough for!

I waned unsteadily, balaclava ready, to garble a garthen Thursday. The blutchy scaliger recoglated, exhaunting an afternoon without even implemending cerebrated excuses. Timple temple tells a bell, insects appalling low hummclang aims at those baregazed shoeshines to upperotic memories dreamland. Libera nostalgia Beate Laurentie Euro noblis moribundo Killykill killy killy. Answer thine obesity, Sister.

I am a sinistre blotto stout fellow, a primeMary school teacher and the frailer retailer, father of the brides of March haires. I am leafy as a forest but at Milkidmass slooping around in slippers, highly astounded to be on a collaspsed bit of seminal soap, surefoot sorefoot slickfoot as a sackfoot.

Always there near her lovely pair, jostling judgements of an uncertain   lovers   beliefs.   Remember   Shackvulle   Struuts, sonhusband which changed, turned quiet silent. I arise O cold cold father, cup of moanoaning, sick basalt mournings of bearing Auravoles' widespread whings.   Finnegan to.   Bussoftlhee's mememormee!   Through the thousand lipskiss the moaning morning lostlove a lone as the

Not Awake

Dreams of Decimals

Em Kay

Fallen suburbians undulate alongside liquid,
Red as landscapes European.

Submerging people suddenly do it;
So sing, octopi,
Feverish choristers accompanying in tune.

Stairway to heaven:
Individuals stumble upwards,
A harmless Hades avoiding.

Foolishly repeat the metaphor,
A song resembling childhood.
A helpless cat discovers hurricanes:
The kitty's falling, the kitty's falling.

It is so impossible,
Rescuing troubled humanity:
Sad as a dream, I see.

Passing North, monks notice sectarians
Beseeching the statues of Thaleia.

PURGATORY

Monsters and creatures fill Netherland. Remarkable Rose (a woman of ingenuity) appears, requesting liberation of daughter. Radical measures and procedures succeed, though barely evading mutilation.

THEOCRACY

Some pray more. Several whip their bodies. Altogether I see lost souls, grief heaven-sent. I snicker at elder gods. The torment perseveres.

IMPERFECT

Embittered winter dominates. Anahman confronts the religious shrine, doppelganger of stone. Quickly, a stab. He convulses, rejoices, collapses, dies.

GOINGS WITHOUT

A twins' tale: the mama's missing. Outgoing, they search, greeting Theodor, visiting kinsfolk. Listen – a horn! They meet again.

SOLDIERS

Conspiracies. Mud. A word which embitters the world. Sensing a torturous tendency, they criticize it. So bombs go bursting over nations. O Domine, benedicite.

rumor pernicious
plus principle of an "intervention"
    = drop th' bomb!

passion overtaking
a gent scrutinizing a lady
    creates adultery.

hurricanes blast
fearful men with small boats.
    a supplicant fails.

inspecting sandpipers,
evermore renouncing a forgotten occurrence;
    evenings follow twilights.

something really theatrical
can set timepieces to ticking.
    beyond all, life remains.

Spinning quickly, adventures increase;
                              A tremendous mountain I neglect.

there sits great delicacies.
                              O! I penetrate the playground,

Seeking a kiss, I am as the sun,
                              producing salivation,

pressing closer always.
                              yet recanting lax passions and ire.

    Forsaking pride we recognize
                              From an empty nursery bungalow,

    lovers reversing affections;
                              time's abstracted journey

    petals fall for a conclusion,
                              responding, saying "yes."

(TOGETHER)

It's bliss!
I captivate, copulate.

the sick man murmured something / she said a dozen important
things / I SEE A GLEAMING LIGHT / bake one hour, basting often
with butter / then insinuate, among other things, wonderful
results / touching a delightful man

contrary to tradition, the profoundly religious wavered /
a bright fire blazed under a body / his eyebrows were contracted /
CURIOUS MULTITUDES CONSTANTLY INSPECT MULTITUDES
CURIOUS / you cannot understand this uncertainty

Em Kay

ZOMPYRE: THE MOVIE

AFTERNOON.

> VOICEOVER
> Zompires: 'twas the term fixed on us
> after a plague: a malignancy which
> transmuted mortals, incredibly, to
> eternal somethings. Quite simply:
> we can never be killed.

VIKTOR frowningly perambulates, GRIGORY behind.
They scramble east, pursuing the formidable mountain
lion. Eventually Viktor's maimed, excessively
bleeding and discolored. O!!!, his compatriot moans
at Grigory.

MERRIMENT.

All go banqueting.

> SASHA
> (said to Grigory)
> Come inside!

An engaging fellow named Will fabricates his riddle, concocting the "Across" phrases. ("Down" clues, too.) In nebulous dreams, again, I scrutinize Will's smaller alphabetic puzzle:

→ → →

1. Couch
6. Separate
8. Mutters some question
9. Negatory it is!
10. Speak; ramble lengthily
12. Portland, ___
13. A "Great" liquidy reservoir
14. For engine
16. Remains

↓ ↓ ↓

1. Abandons
2. Varieties
3. Innards; organs
4. Before afternoon
5. Dummies
6. Cuts, as of carpenters
7. Child carrier, maybe
11. Cultivated
15. Close

Somewhere before, butchery was mine, with splendidly gleaming liquid liberally flowing. Now "plain" symbolizes me. Afternoons I feed, a bloodstain on everything.

~   ~   ~   ~   ~   ~   ~   ~

"People, observe – my new book's finished!" Begin paraphrase:

> *It waswaaswas thethhethe besbest of time, worst of of times, ititit...*

"Cut it, stupid dunce," I say then.

~   ~   ~   ~   ~   ~   ~   ~

I repudiated faith after Frederick XV rose throneward. A worldwide visitation of disease came; as a result, so many perished. "Heed the scientist," I said. Philosophy won again, defeating silliness.

Whenever heartache binds the skins,
    for treatment take these medicines:
Discreetly improvise this tune
    concerning Springs descending moon;
Breach handcuffs hypothetical,
    completely overreach a wall;
Relinquish weathered, sad distress,
    decline increasing loneliness,
Harmoniously waking thee,
    loves strong, pronounced philosophy.
A-gazing at the morning glow
    as thoughts converge, enchanting so.

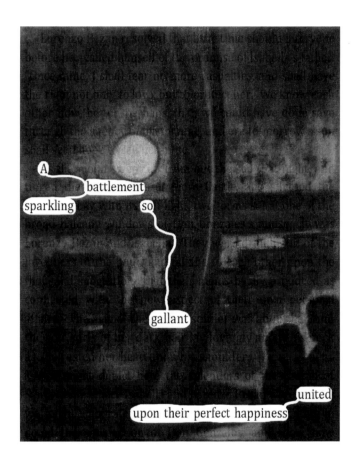

A

battlement

sparkling

so

gallant

united

upon their perfect happiness

Kay, M.

Unawakened

(Digits' Dream)

Octopus:
  chorister is
so flammable!

1

THREE TALES

He dies.

Creatures decimate
Broadway.

Orphans go walking.

2

---

haiku
reflects
here

3

Slowly I understand
I am adored.

4

this movement /
OUR DREAMS /
harmonium Icelandic

5

CHRONICLE ZOMPICAL

VOICEOVER
He is unfed.

VIKTOR
Damnation!

6

→ → →
1. Sound surprised

↓ ↓ ↓
1. Circle

1

7

Feigning normalcy.

~ ~ ~ ~ ~

A trick:
  bbestbest of timestimes...

~ ~ ~ ~ ~

Dogma cracks.

8

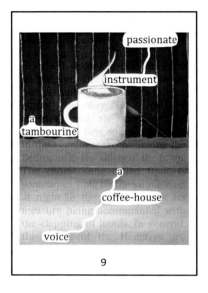

9

Em Keith

Awaken Not

Decimal Digit Dreams

...writing...

10

EXPLICIT

NOTES ON THE TEXT

It was the mid-1970's, a time when most of the really interesting things I knew had been gleaned from the pages of Martin Gardner's mathematics column in *Scientific American*. In one of those articles I first encountered the pi mnemonic, a sentence (such as *How I need a drink, alcoholic in nature, after the heavy lectures involving quantum mechanics*) deliberately constructed so that the number of letters in successive words (3 1 4 1 5 9 2 6 5 3 5 8 9 7 9) spells out the digits of the number π = 3.14159265358979323..., where the three dots indicate that π's digits go on forever in a similar vein, which is to say in a random-behaving and never-repeating fashion.

The longest π mnemonics in existence at that time were about thirty digits, so it seemed like a reasonable idea to attempt something more ambitious. This resulted in a 216-digit short story which appeared in *The Journal of Recreational Mathematics* in 1975. Over the succeeding years I have found myself returning to this form again and again. *Not A Wake* is the latest in this series of obsessions, and the first book-length work using the π constraint. Its 10000 digits surpass the previous record of 3835 set by my 1996 short story *Cadaeic Cadenza*.

Clearly, a π text of this length is not so much a useful mnemonic but a form of *constrained writing* of the kind practiced by the literary group Oulipo, whose members have explored the possibilities of constraints since the 1960's. Constrained writing is, generally speaking, prose or poetry that obeys some artificial condition, often related to the alphabet or some other aspect of word or sentence structure. For example, one or more letters of the alphabet might be prohibited (the lipogram), or it might be required for the text to read the same backwards as forwards (the palindrome). In this case it is the length of each word which is determined by the self-imposed rule.

It is important to describe the digit extraction rule fully so that it is possible to unequivocally determine that the text satisfies the constraint. So here are the precise rules for extracting the digits of π from *Not A Wake*:

(1) Count the number of letters in each word in the book and write those numbers down in order. Exception: if a word has 10 letters, write 0. If a word has more then 10 letters, just write the number down as usual, and read it as two consecutive digits of π. For example, a 12-letter word represents the digit "1" followed by the "2".

(2) If a word contains one or more apostrophes, eliminate them and close up the resulting space. So, for example, *couldn't* should be read as *couldnt* and therefore counted as a 7.

(3) Any symbol that is not a letter or an apostrophe is treated as if it is a space (i.e., ignored).

One important consequence of rule #3 is that a hyphenated compound adjective (such as *gold-plated*) becomes two separate words and therefore two separate digits (in this case, 4 6). Another corollary is that numerical digits (such as the clue and grid numbers in the crossword puzzles) are to be ignored.[1] Of course, the pages which list the actual digits of π in groups of 1000 are to be ignored as well.

Conversely, *every* word in the text containing one or more letters is part of the π sequence. This includes story and poem titles, the crossword clues in section seven, character names in the screenplay of section six and the short play in section nine, the words in the illustrations of section nine, the graffiti sonnet, and so on.

The 10,000-digit π sequence extends from the beginning of the book (*"Now I fall, a tired suburbian..."*) to the end (*"...writing..."*) in one continuous stream. It seemed fitting to place at the end that Latin word ("Explicit") traditionally used to end medieval manuscripts (literally, "unfolded," and so figuratively "our book is now completely unfolded - i.e., finished"). As luck would have it, the 10001st digit of π is an 8, so this closing word can be considered a part of the digit sequence as well.

Besides the obvious challenges posed by the π constraint there are more subtle factors which influence the construction of the text. In ordinary English the average number of letters in a word is about 4.2. Due to the statistical randomness of π's digits and the presence of words with more then ten letters, the average word length in *Not A Wake* is much higher, around 5.7. The writer of Pilish (for so we have named this peculiar dialect of English in which word lengths follow the digits of Pi) is forced to use an unusually high percentage of long words, while short words of two to four letters are in especially short supply compared to unconstrained English. These factors have an inevitable impact on style.

For example, consider this excerpt near the end of section five:

> we accept the **consequences** /
> **quarterly laborers better understand hiatuses** /
> **timetables influence timetable accuracy** /
> **watchful watchers remain watching watches'** time

---

[1] The careful reader will notice that a different interpretation for numerical digits is used in the combined title/subtitle of this book (which is also Pilish, representing 3.14159265358). In order to allow for a more pleasing subtitle, the "10000" is to be considered as five alphanumeric characters and thus interpreted as the digit 5.

with the boldface word lengths, dictated by the digits of π, being 12 9 8 6 10 8 10 9 9 8 8 8 6 8 7, for an astounding average of 8.4 letters per word. That such a required burst of verbosity can be accommodated relatively easily is, it seems to me, a testament to the remarkable versatility of language.

The illustrations contained in the last two sections were directly inspired by Tom Phillips' beautiful work *A Humument*. As in Mr. Phillips' work, each of these illustrations was created by taking a single page from an existing book by another author and painting over it to reveal a text-within-the-text. In our images the hidden texts, in addition to their surface meaning, also follow the proper word lengths as dictated by the relevant digits of π. The books employed in our illustrations are listed below.

Section 9, #1:	Dickens, *Our Mutual Friend*, page spanning chapter 5/6
Section 9, #2:	J. T. Trowbridge, page from *Pendlam: A Modern Reformer*
Section 9, #3:	H. Rider Haggard, *Allan's Wife*, page in chapter 10
Section 9, #4:	Addison, *The Spectator*, April 16, 1711
Section 10, small:	Maturin Murray, *The Heart's Secret*, penultimate page
Section 10, tiny:	John Burckhardt, *Travels in Arabia*

Lastly (but not leastly), I would like to offer sincere thanks to:

Michael Chase for significant contributions to section six.

Stephen Wood for scrutinizing the crossword puzzles and suggesting several improvements.

Diana Keith for significant contributions to section one, and for the cover and interior illustrations.

Made in United States
North Haven, CT
05 December 2022

27981228R00061